The Library
SHELVES

AN INTERACTIVE MYSTERY ADVENTURE

by Steve Brezenoff
illustrated by Marcos Calo

Field Trip Mysteries Adventures
are published by Stone Arch Books
a Capstone Imprint
1710 Roe Crest Drive
North Mankato, Minnesota 56003
www.mycapstone.com

Library of Congress Cataloging-in-Publication Data is available on the
Library of Congress website.

978-1-4965-4860-3 (hardcover)
978-1-4965-4862-7 (paperback)
978-1-4965-4864-1 (eBook PDF)

Graphic Designer: Bobbie Nuytten
Editor: Hank Musolf
Production Specialist: Laura Manthe

When something is scratching the inside of the vents in the library,
junior detectives Sam, Egg, Gum, and Cat are on the case!

Printed in the United States of America.
PA49

YOU CHOOSE STORIES

A FIELD TRIP MYSTERIES ADVENTURE

The Library SHELVES

STONE ARCH BOOKS
a capstone imprint

Catalina Duran

A.K.A.: Cat

BIRTHDAY: February 1

LEVEL: 6th Grade

INTERESTS:

Animals, being "gre

field trips

Edward G. Garrison

A.K.A.: Egg

BIRTHDAY: May 14th

LEVEL: 6th Grade

INTERESTS:

Photography, field trip

James Shoo

A.K.A.: Gum

BIRTHDAY: November 19th

LEVEL: 6th Grade

INTERESTS:
Gum-chewing, field trips, and showing everyone what a crook Anton Gutman is

Samantha Archer

A.K.A.: Sam

BIRTHDAY: August 20th

LEVEL: 6th Grade

INTERESTS:
Old movies, field trips

FIELD TRIP MYSTERIES

Mr. Spade's sixth-grade class arrives at the River City Central Library just after nine in the morning. "Not a single computer open," says James Shoo, better known to his friends as Gum. "How am I supposed to play *Blast 'Em Arena* without a computer?"

"We're not here to play video games, Gum," says Catalina Duran. "We're here to learn about libraries."

"What's to learn, Cat?" Samantha Archer throws up her hands. "We've all been coming to libraries since we were babies. They're quiet. They have lots of books."

Beside her, Edward G. Garrison—or Egg— snaps a photo of the big front hall. It has sculptures, huge columns, marble stairways, and glittering chandeliers.

TURN THE PAGE.

"There's more to a library than books, Sam," Egg says.

"Like what?" Sam says. She puts her hands on her hips and smirks.

Sam might be his best friend, but she's also the tallest girl in sixth grade.

She's a tiny bit intimidating.

"They have a lot of programs for the community here," Egg says. "Story time for little kids, sessions on researching online . . . my grandmother comes to this branch for her motorcycle repair class."

"There won't be any of that today," Mr. Spade says as he steps up to the four friends. "In fact, the librarian will mostly talk to us about the history of the building itself."

"Mr. Spade!" says a voice. The voice is loud in the quiet front atrium of the library. Everyone turns to look. The voice belongs to a tall, slim man in a baggy, tan suit. "Sorry I'm late. Crazy morning here at the library—as usual!"

His smile is big and bright, and he shakes Mr. Spade's hand with vigor. "Thank you for coming," he says. "My favorite part of the job as branch community relations director is giving tours to local youth."

"You must be Mr. Burhan," Mr. Spade says.

"Please! Call me Abdi," says the man.

"Abdi it is," Mr. Spade says as Abdi finally releases his hand.

"Abdi might want to switch to decaf," Gum whispers to Cat. She gives him a gentle shove.

"So, boys and girls," Abdi says, "who's ready to start our tour?"

A few limp hands go up, along with a few kids quietly saying "me."

"Then let's go!" Abdi says.

But Cat raises her hand. "Mr. Burhan?"

"Please!" he says. "Call me Abdi."

"Will we have a chance to check out books too?" Cat asks.

TURN THE PAGE.

"Of course!" Abdi says, laughing. "Libraries have changed a lot in the last few decades, but we still do love books!"

"Good," Cat whispers to her friends. "I have to get the newest book in the Elves and Spells series. Jasper said it's the best one yet."

Jasper Farmhill is another student in Mr. Spade's sixth-grade class. He's the biggest bookworm, especially when it comes to fantasy stories, like the Elves and Spells series by Deirdre Black.

Abdi leads the kids into an old part of the building. It has columns, a dome ceiling, and fancy-looking portraits on the walls. "Not many of our patrons spend time in this part of the library," Abdi admits. "It houses our special collection, and—"

He stops suddenly and cocks his head as if trying to hear. His suit jacket flutters in the cold breeze of an air-conditioner vent.

"Does anyone else hear that?" Abdi asks.

"The only thing I heard was the tour guide admitting how boring this place is," Sam whispers to Gum.

"I hear it," Cat says. "A scratching sound."

Abdi nods. "That's it," he says. "Oh, I hope we don't have vermin in the ducts again."

A few kids gasp.

"I don't mean again," Abdi says. "Why would it be again? We've never had vermin. Follow me!"

Abdi hurries from the room. The four friends follow but stop as the class leaves. They linger near the air-conditioning vent.

"I hear it now," Sam says. "Sounds like it might be claws scratching in there."

"Maybe it's raccoons?" Cat suggests.

They hurry after the tour and join Jasper at the back of the pack as Abdi leads them into an especially colorful room. "This is my favorite section," Abdi says. "I hope you're all familiar with this room, the children's literature section!"

TURN THE PAGE.

"We'll spend a few minutes here," Mr. Spade says. "Here's a good chance to choose a few titles to check out." Cat hurries to the fiction middle grade shelves. "Let's see," she says. Her three best friends look as she pushes books aside, looking for the one she wants. "They're not here. Not a single book from the Elves and Spells series."

"Jasper probably checked them all out," Gum suggests.

"Maybe . . ." Cat says.

Gum spots Jasper a few shelves over. "Hey, Jasper," he says, "Do you have all the Elves and Spells books?"

"I don't have any of them," Jasper says. "At least not from the library. I own a boxed set, signed by the author, if you must know."

"Of course you do," Gum says.

"But I did see the entire series on the shelf," Jasper says.

"That can't be!" Cat says. "I just looked. There are none there."

TURN THE PAGE.

"Not that shelf," Jasper says. He points at a shelf standing all alone in the middle of the room. "That shelf."

The sign above it reads "Holds."

"What does 'holds' mean?" Sam says.

"I hope it means I can still check out the new one," Cat says.

Cat scoops up the most recent title.

An older woman seated nearby clucks her tongue. Cat glances at her.

"Oh, sorry! Those aren't for you," says a girl's voice.

Cat spins around. The girl is a little taller than Sam, and she has curly brown hair bunched into a top knot. Her cat glasses give her the air of a true librarian—except she can't be more than sixteen years old.

"That's where we put books that patrons have requested," she says. "That way they have a couple of days to get down here and claim the book and no one else can check them out."

"I didn't know you could do that," Cat says. She hugs the book to herself. "No one told me!"

"I just told you," the girl says as she snatches the book back. She places it back on the holds shelf and walks away, pushing a metal cart full of books.

Abdi laughs lightly as he steps up to Cat. "Don't mind her," he whispers. "That's Yasmin. She volunteers here three afternoons a week as part of a class at her high school."

"Oh," Cat says. "She takes her job very seriously."

"Indeed," Abdi says. "I'll be happy to put you on the hold list for the entire Elves and Spells series. Do you have your library card with you?"

Cat pulls her card from her back pocket. "Right here," she says.

"Come with me to the desk and—oh no," Abdi says, cutting himself off. He snatches a slip of yellow paper from a nearby shelf. "Not another one."

TURN THE PAGE.

"Another what?" Sam asks. She can smell a mystery, and she wants to solve it.

"Oh, it's nothing, I'm sure," Abdi says. "But someone has been grabbing scrap paper from the basket on my reservations desk and sticking it into books all over the library."

"Sounds mysterious," Sam says, rubbing her palms together.

"Yeah, real mysterious," Gum says. "Library visitors using scraps of paper as bookmarks! I'll call the police!"

Sam snarls at him and crosses her arms.

"I'm sure it's harmless," Abdi says as he crumples the paper in his fist. "I just don't like to find scraps of paper around." He tosses the paper into a nearby trash can.

The moment Abdi walks away, Sam grabs the scrap of paper and unballs it. In thick, black marker is written LEO I.

"This doesn't make sense," she says. "'LEO I'. What does that mean?"

"Nah," Gum says. "It just says 'lee-oy.'"

"What does that mean?" Cat asks.

Egg takes the paper from Sam. "'Leo one', maybe? Like Roman numerals."

"Young lady?" Abdi calls from the nearby desk. "Your library card?"

"Oh, right," Cat says. "Sorry. Coming!" She hurries to the desk to reserve the books.

"I'll just scan your card and—oh," Abdi says, glancing at the computer screen in front of him. "How odd."

"Huh?" Cat says. "Something wrong with my card? I never return things late."

Abdi laughs. "Indeed," he says. "Your record is spotless. It's about the series, Elves and Spells. It seems the whole series is on hold and has been for . . . well, forever."

"What do you mean?" Cat asks.

Abdi clicks around on his computer for a few moments before responding.

TURN THE PAGE.

"It seems a library patron has been reserving these books every week since the first book came out three years ago," Abdi says. "How have I never noticed this before?"

"I guess they're a slow reader," Cat says.

"But that's the weirdest part," Abdi says. "She's never even picked them up."

"In three years?" Cat asks. "And they stay on the hold shelf forever?"

Abdi shakes his head. "No, we hold a book for only one week," he says. "But there is no limit on how many times you can put a hold on a book. So in theory . . ."

"If no one else grabs a book, it can go right back onto the hold shelf," Cat finishes for him.

"Exactly," Abdi says. "Ah well, you're next. When the current hold expires, we'll send you an email and you can come pick up the books."

"Thank you!" Cat chirps.

She hurries back to her friends. "You guys have to hear this!" she says.

"What is it?" Egg asks.

"I've got a mystery about Elves and Spells." Cat says.

"Get in line," Gum says. "The scratching in the vents is more important. It's probably an alien infestation."

"Don't be goofy," Sam says. "These nonsense notes are proof of an international spy ring! We have to solve this mystery and quick or this whole joint might be in for it."

TO INVESTIGATE WHO HAS THE ELVES AND SPELLS BOOKS, TURN TO PAGE 20.
TO TRY AND FIND OUT WHAT'S SCRATCHING IN THE VENTS, TURN TO PAGE 50.
TO TRY AND SOLVE THE NONSENSE NOTES, TURN TO PAGE 81.

"I don't see what the big mystery is," Gum says. The four sleuthing friends are sitting in the teen reading nook. It's the only place they can speak privately about the case.

"It's obviously Jasper," Gum adds. "Everyone knows he loves those books."

Cat shakes her head. "He has his own copies," she says. "Besides, Abdi said it was a girl."

"You asked?" Egg says, surprised.

"No, but Abdi said 'she,'" Cat explains.

"Good observation," Sam says. She scribbles in her clues notebook: female.

Gum stands and stretches. "This is silly," he says. "Come on."

He walks up to the desk to Abdi.

"Gum, wait," Cat calls after him in an urgent whisper.

But Gum doesn't wait. His friends hurry after him.

"Hey, Mister Librarian," Gum says. "Who has all the Elves and Spells books on hold?"

Abdi laughs. "Oh, I can't tell you that," he says. "The library takes every patron's privacy very seriously."

"Even about some silly fantasy books?" Gum says.

"About every book," Abdi says. "It's not up to me to decide which patrons deserve privacy and about which subjects."

"I guess . . . ," Gum says. "Thanks anyway."

He and his friends wander away from the desk.

"I was about to tell you," Cat says. "Librarians are very passionate about privacy."

"I think he seems suspicious," Gum says. "Put him on your suspects list, Sam."

"He runs the place!" Sam protests.

Gum thinks a moment. "What are those three things we're supposed to know before we bust someone?" he asks.

"Three things?" Sam says. "Oh, 'means, motive, and opportunity,' you mean?"

TURN THE PAGE.

"That's it," Gum says. "Well, Abdi has two of those already. You got a better suspect?"

"No," Egg says, "but he's not a 'she.'"

Gum rolls his eyes back. "We got that information from him," Gum points out. "He could have just said that to throw Cat off the trail."

Cat, who has already grown fond of the librarian, crosses her arms. "And what do you suggest for motive?" she asks.

"Who knows!" Gum says, throwing up his arms. "Maybe he wants to keep them off the shelves so you can't get them."

Sam scribbles in her notebook.

"Samantha Archer," Cat says, "please tell me you're not writing that down."

"It is a possible motive," Sam says.

"What do you mean?" Egg says.

"Look at Jasper over there," Sam says, nodding toward their classmate.

Jasper sits alone at a table by the window. It's quiet and serene. The only other person in the corner is the older woman with red hair they saw earlier. She is reading a thin pamphlet. The cover says something about magic and books.

Jasper sits with a small stack of books. One book lies open in front of him.

"That kid loves books," Sam says.

"Obviously," Gum says.

"And what would we assume about a kid who reserves a big series like Elves and Spells?" Sam asks.

"That she loves books too," Cat says.

"Naturally," Sam says. She paces in front of her three best friends, her hands clasped around the notebook behind her back. "But what if the culprit is a girl who hates books?"

"Then she wouldn't reserve them?" Egg tries.

"Unless she wanted to be sure no one would read them," Sam explained.

To investigate someone who loves books, turn to page 24.
To investigate someone who hates books, turn to page 30.

With Cat and Egg close behind, Sam and Gum step up to Jasper's table.

"Jasper," Sam says, "do you know anyone else who loves the Elves and Spells books as much as you? Besides Cat, I mean."

"Sure," Jasper says. "I know Chloe is pretty obsessed with it. She draws fan art constantly."

Chloe Marshfield—the class artist.

"I didn't know Chloe liked books," Sam says. She taps her chin as her gaze wanders the room.

Chloe is never too hard to find. She keeps her short hair dyed bright blue. But there's no sign of her in this reading room.

"Sure she does," Jasper says. He gets back to his reading, adding quickly, "As long as there are good illustrations."

"Have you seen her today?" Sam asks.

Jasper shakes his head. He's barely listening anymore. His mind is right back on the story in front of him.

"She was on the bus," Cat says as the four sleuths leave the big reading room. "But I didn't see her when we all met Abdi."

"Then she snuck off pretty quickly," Sam concludes.

"Maybe to check the hold shelf," Gum says.

The four sleuths walk down a long, quiet corridor.

Egg raises his camera and snaps a photo of the hallway in front of them. At the end of the hall is a wide window that climbs from a built-in bench right up to the high ceiling.

Lounging on the bench with the sun behind her and a sketchbook on her lap is Chloe. A vent near her head makes her short blue hair flutter.

"You better do the talking, Cat," Sam whispers as the four friends step up to Chloe. "She trusts you."

Chloe and Cat have been friendly this school year, at least more so than Chloe and the others.

"Hi, Chloe," Cat says.

TURN THE PAGE.

"Uh-oh," Chloe says. "Looks like I'm a suspect."

All four detectives stand there a moment, mouths open to talk, but only Sam thinks of something to say.

"Suspect?" she says, grinning. "Has there been a crime?"

"Ooh, sounds like I know too much already," Chloe says, smiling to herself and still sketching on her pad. "Better call the coppers on me."

"Oh stop," Cat says, forcing a giggle. "You're not a suspect."

"What?" Gum says. He grabs Sam's pad out of her hand. "It says it right here: 'Suspects: Jasper, Abdi, Chloe . . .' See?"

Chloe laughs. The chilly air from the vent beside her blows her bangs over her eyes and she pushes them back.

"You four are fun," she says. "But anyway, you've got the wrong girl. I didn't put a hold on those Elves and Spells books."

TURN THE PAGE.

"How did you—," Cat starts.

"You forget," Chloe says, finally looking up from her drawing. "You detectives might be great at investigating, but we artists are better at observing. I've observed you four all morning."

"All right, smarty," Sam says, crossing her arms. "Got an alibi?"

"Nope," Chloe says. "Got a motive?"

"Jasper said you love the Elves and Spells series," Sam says.

"I do," Chloe replies. "Amazing art by Marcos Calo. Who wouldn't love them? But that's not a motive. Take a look in my satchel."

She nods toward the faded and soft-looking leather shoulder bag on the floor next to the bench.

Cat squats and opens the flap. Inside—along with loads of pencils and pens and brushes and paper—is a paperback set of Elves and Spells books, including most of the ones on the hold shelf.

"I think she's innocent," Cat says. "Sorry, Chloe."

"No apologies necessary," Chloe says. "Good luck with your case."

"Now what?" Gum says.

"Now I believe it's time for me to say thank you," Abdi says, suddenly standing over the sleuths, "for visiting the library today. I think your teacher Mr. Spade is gathering the students to get back on the bus."

"Back on the bus?" Sam says, "But we've barely started!"

"There's always next time, kids," Mr. Spade says when the four sleuths join the rest of their class. "This library has so much more than you can see in only one visit."

THE END

TO FOLLOW ANOTHER PATH, TURN TO PAGE 19.

Sam leads her friends toward Jasper's table near the window, but she stops around the corner and peeks around.

"Watch this," she says.

As they spy, a girl from their class sits down across from Jasper.

"Bernice Warren," Gum says. "They're best friends. Have been forever."

"Hi, Jasper," Bernice says.

Jasper doesn't look up from his book.

"What are you reading?" Bernice asks.

Jasper still doesn't look up. He looks like nothing could pull him away from his story.

"Oh, really?" Bernice says. "What's it about? . . . Dorks? It's about dorks? . . . Oh, just one dork who likes to ignore his best friend all the time? Sounds really dumb."

Jasper goes right on reading.

"It's like he doesn't even know she's there," Cat says. "Poor Bernice."

"Okay," Bernice says in a huff as she stands up. "Bye, I guess."

With that, the girl walks away looking angry. Jasper doesn't seem to realize he had a visitor at all.

The four sleuths retreat around the corner and fully out of sight. Sam scribbles in her notebook, recording the scene they just witnessed.

"What do you think?" Sam says. "Strong theory, huh? She has motive. And means. Anyone with a library card can put a hold on a book online."

"Plenty of opportunity," Egg says. Cat, meanwhile, stares into space and chews on her pencil.

"Penny for your thoughts, Cat?" Sam says.

"Jasper is a friend of mine," Cat says. "And I think he's being downright rude to Bernice. I'll go talk to him right now."

TURN THE PAGE.

Cat nods once, as if to convince herself it's the right thing to do. Then she stalks around the corner and over to Jasper's table.

Her three friends hurry behind her but still keep their distance.

"Jasper," Cat says, putting a firm hand on his shoulder to get his attention, "I want you to know that you were just very rude to Bernice."

"Bernice?" Jasper says. "I haven't seen her since we got off the bus."

"She was just sitting with you," Cat explains. "You ignored her!"

"I must have been so interested in the book," Jasper says. He sags in his seat. "That's been happening a lot lately. I'll apologize to her."

He grabs his books and jumps up to follow her. He stops suddenly and turns to Cat. "She doesn't understand," he says, smiling. "Bernice isn't much of a reader. She doesn't even have a library card."

With that, Jasper hurries away.

The older woman with the thin pamphlet looks up a moment and grins at Cat. She nods, far more pleasant than she was earlier when she shook her head at Cat and clucked her tongue. As she walks off, she lays her pamphlet on the table. The cover says "Magic in Books: A Warning."

"Who made her the library manners police?" Gum whispers as he picks up the pamphlet. "Ooh, magic."

"It's fine," Cat says. "But did you hear what Jasper said?"

Gum nods. Sam and Egg walk up. Egg snaps a photo of the dusty-light corner. Sam scratches some notes down in her book.

"So what do you think?" Cat asks.

IF IT WAS DEFINITELY BERNICE, TURN TO PAGE 34.
IF IT WAS DEFINITELY NOT BERNICE, TURN TO PAGE 41.

The four sleuths gather in the long, quiet hallway outside the big reading room. Bernice is close to the main entrance. She is leaning on the wall and looking at her feet.

"There she is," Cat says, her voice a little sad. "Poor girl. Jasper sure was rude to her."

"So what are we waiting for?" Gum says. With that, he pops a piece of cucumber-watermelon-mint gum into his mouth and leads the other sleuths down the hall toward Bernice.

"What do you want?" Bernice says, glaring at the approaching detectives.

Gum opens his mouth to talk, but Cat silences him with a hand on his arm.

"We just wanted to see if you were OK," Cat says. "We saw how rude Jasper was to you."

"I'm fine," Bernice says. "Who cares about Jasper anyway?"

"You do," Egg points out.

Bernice shrugs. "So?" she says. "We're not friends anymore. I don't care."

"Of course," Sam says as she casually drapes an arm over the girl's shoulders. "Who would care? All he ever does is read."

"Exactly," Bernice says. "It's so boring."

"Tell me about it," Sam says. "Cat's the same way. Such a bore."

"Right?" Bernice says. "He's always asking me if I read some dumb book, when I obviously haven't."

"I know," Sam says, shaking her head. She winks quickly at Cat. "So annoying."

"I'm glad someone understands," Bernice says with a nod.

"You know," Sam says, and she leans down to say quietly in Bernice's ear, "someone should make sure these dorks can never read the books they love."

"What do you mean?" Bernice asks.

"What if we figured a way to make it so no one could read the Elves and Spells series," Sam says, "ever again?"

TURN THE PAGE.

Bernice gasps and backs away from Sam. "Wait a minute," she says. "What are you—?"

"Aha!" Sam says. "So it *was* you!"

"What was me?" Bernice says with a look of shock.

"Oh, please," Sam says with a wave of her hand. "The look on your face says it all."

Gum nods. "Guilty," he says. "No doubt."

"No!" Bernice says, putting her hands in front of her and backing away. "I just meant . . ."

"Yes?" Sam says. "What did you mean?"

"Just . . . how awful!" Bernice says.

"What?" Sam says, stunned.

"I mean, Jasper is my best friend!" Bernice says. Her voice echoes up and down the empty hallway.

"Right, but you said—," Sam says.

Bernice cuts her off. "I was upset!" Bernice says. "I still wouldn't do that to Jasper. He'd be miserable! And so would Cat!"

TURN THE PAGE.

Cat's eyes go wide. "Leave me out of this," she says.

"Isn't Sam your best friend?" Bernice says, flicking her glare at Cat.

"Well, yes . . . ," Cat stammers.

"Can you believe what she suggested?" Bernice says.

"I think she was just—," Cat begins.

"It's unthinkable!" Bernice says. "Keeping so many children from their greatest pleasure. What a monster you are, Sam!" she adds.

"So you didn't put a hold on the whole Elves and Spells series," Egg says, "to prevent anyone else from doing what Jasper did to you?"

"Of course I didn't," Bernice says, "but if that's what this is all about then it makes a little more sense now. I'm sorry for shouting at you, Sam."

"It's okay," Sam says.

"I can't believe you think I would do something like that, though," Bernice says.

"Well, obviously you would never," Sam admits, "after that rant."

"I mean," Bernice says, "it's a pretty smart idea. But I couldn't anyway, and not just because Jasper is my bestie. You need a library card to put something on hold."

"And you don't have one," Cat says, nodding. "Jasper told us. I forgot."

Bernice shrugs. "Sorry, guys," she says. "I better go try again with Jasper. Thanks for helping me see how important he is to me."

"Sure," Sam says. "Anytime!"

"Now what?" Gum says. "Bernice was a bust."

"Maybe it's time for you four to do some reading," Mr. Spade says.

Mr. Spade stands over the detectives.

"We were just talking to—," Sam says.

"You were snooping around," Mr. Spade says. "I think for the rest of the trip you four should sit with me."

TURN THE PAGE.

"The rest of the trip?" Sam says, distraught as Mr. Spade waves them over. "Then we won't have time to find the real culprit!"

"Sorry, gang," Mr. Spade says when the four sleuths join the rest of their class. "Can't solve 'em all."

THE END

To follow another path, turn to page 19.

"I don't think it was Bernice," Cat says as the four sleuths leave the reading room and step into the long and quiet hallway.

At one end, their classmate Chloe sits on a bench in a window and draws in her sketchbook. The air from a nearby vent blows across her head, making her hair flick wildly.

At the other end, Bernice leans on the wall and looks sadly at her shoes.

"Right," Sam says, looking at her notebook. "No library card. She couldn't put anything on hold, even if she does have a pretty good motive to take Elves and Spells out of circulation."

"Now what?" Egg asks.

"What about this?" Gum says, holding up a slim booklet. "This pamphlet actually mentions the Elves and Spells series."

Sam snatches it from his fingers. "Huh," she says. "This pamphlet is all about fantasy stories for kids, especially Elves and Spells."

"What about them?" Cat asks.

Turn the page.

Sam scans the text. "It seems to say that books like E and S," she explains, "are a bad influence for young readers."

"That's ridiculous," Cat says.

"I've heard about this," Egg says. "A group of people who think magic is bad for kids are trying to get the series banned from public libraries and schools."

"Where did you get this?" Sam asks as she folds the thin little pamphlet.

Gum chews thoughtfully. He blows a little green bubble and it pops, sticking to his lips. Finally, he shrugs. "I don't remember," he says.

"Great," Cat says. "A dead end."

"Gum, try to remember," Egg says.

IF IT BELONGED TO AN OLDER WOMAN IN THE LIBRARY, CONTINUE ON TO PAGE 43.

IF IT WAS STICKING OUT FROM BETWEEN TWO BOOKS ON A SHELF, TURN TO PAGE 48.

"I got it from her," Gum says. "I'm sure of it."

The four sleuths are mostly hidden among the stacks as they watch a woman seated on a bench not far from the hold shelf. Sam leads the others across the room and stops in front of the woman.

"Excuse me, ma'am," Sam says.

The woman looks up from her phone. A pin on the lapel of her blazer says "Magic is Evil, Sinister Stuff."

"Yes?" she says.

"Is this yours?" Sam asks. She holds up the pamphlet Gum found.

"It was mine," the woman says. "I have a stack of them." She pats the bulky purse in her lap.

"I leave them here and there," she says, "in the hope that some open-minded parent will pick one up and join our mission. Did you read it?"

"We sure did," Sam says.

"Wonderful," the woman says, standing up. "Now, if you'll excuse me—"

TURN THE PAGE.

"One more thing," Cat says, "I tried to check out the Elves and Spells series this morning. Do you know it?"

"Of course I know it," the woman says, "If our anti-fantasy-book group, Magic is Evil, Sinister Stuff, or M.E.S.S., has our way, it won't even be in this library much longer."

"But it's still here now," Sam says. "I suppose you know why Cat couldn't check it out, though, huh?"

"I certainly do," the woman says. "I've had the whole series on hold for months. I've done nothing wrong."

"Nothing illegal," Cat points out. "But maybe something wrong. If you see what I mean."

"I've never heard something so silly," the woman says. "We've done nothing wrong at all. Several members of M.E.S.S. have reserved the Elves and Spells titles all over the state to ensure that our youth are not getting their hands on those wicked books."

Abdi the librarian walks over to the group.

TURN THE PAGE.

"Everything okay over here?" he asks, smiling.

"Tell them I've done nothing wrong," the woman says.

"She's absolutely right, kids," Abdi says. "She and her fellow M.E.S.S. members used our online reservation system just as intended."

"See?" the woman says.

"Why, we've had so many holds for the Elves and Spells series all over the system," Abdi goes on, his smile growing, "that we've had to order more copies."

"Wait, what?" the woman says, stopping.

"Yes," Abdi says. "I just got off the phone with our buyer, in fact. We're ordering another twenty sets to handle the demand. The publisher says we're the library system with the most copies in the state."

"Huh," Sam says. "I guess this little scheme backfired a bit, didn't it, lady?"

"Oh, how rude," the woman says. She walks off, huffing angrily.

"And that's not all," Abdi says, raising his voice slightly so the woman can still hear. "It seems the publisher is so pleased, they're sending the author, Deirdre Black, herself to this very library for a reading and signing next month."

The woman stops at the exit to the children's books room. She turns to face the four sleuths and their new librarian friend.

"You may cancel my hold, sir," she says. "And you can expect the rest of our members to cancel theirs as well."

With that, she turns and leaves.

"I don't think she'll be back here anytime soon," Egg says, snapping a photo of her walking angrily away.

"And more importantly," Abdi says, turning to Cat, "if you'll take out your library card and come with me, I think there are a few Elves and Spells books that just became available."

THE END

TO FOLLOW ANOTHER PATH, TURN TO PAGE 19.

"Abdi, the librarian guy, told us about these pesky things," Gum says. "He's finding them all over the library."

"Those were just scraps of paper," Egg says. "Not pamphlets like this. There are probably a bunch more just like it."

"Hey, here's one," Cat says. She's a few steps away in the Nonfiction—Biographies section. She pulls out a torn slip of paper from between two books. It's no bigger than a dollar bill.

"What's it say?" Sam asks.

"Yeah," Gum says. "Does it look like this pamphlet I found?" He winks at Egg. "I bet it does," he says.

"Not even a little," Cat calls back. "It just says 'L-E-I.' Looks like someone wrote it in thick, black marker."

"What does 'L-E-I' mean?" Sam says aloud as she writes it in her notebook.

Mr. Spade, who has stepped up to their table without them noticing, coughs into his hand. "You'll have to research that another day," he says. "Time to get back on the bus."

"What?" Gum says. "We're out of time already?"

"'Fraid so," Mr. Spade says. With that, their teacher heads toward the front doors.

"Then the mystery is unsolved," Sam says as she stands. "I don't know what this feeling is, but I don't like it."

Egg pats her on the back as the four failed sleuths follow behind Mr. Spade. "It's disappointment, Sam," he says. "I feel it too."

THE END

TO FOLLOW ANOTHER PATH, TURN TO PAGE 19.

50

"I don't see what the big mystery is," Sam says. "It's probably just raccoons."

The four sleuths have split off from the rest of the class. They walk slowly along a wide corridor trimmed in dark, old wood. Its high ceiling is lit by golden chandeliers between big beams.

A maintenance worker is up on a ladder beneath one of the chandeliers.

At one end of the hall is a built-in bench topped with a firm-looking cushion under a high, paned window.

Cat sits on the bench. Gum sits behind her. Sam stands in front of him with her arms crossed. When Egg reaches them, he stands beside her.

"I can hear it right now," Gum says. He leans close to the vent set into the wall beside him. It's a fancy-looking vent, painted gold and designed to look more like intertwined shoots of ivy and leaves, rather than an ordinary crisscross design.

"It's definitely coming from in there," Egg says, leaning closer.

"I don't know what else can live in air-conditioning ducts besides cute little critters," Cat says.

Cat's favorite animals are cats, of course, but she has a soft spot for furry and fuzzy animals of all species.

Sam paces in front of them. "This does seem pretty simple," she admits. "And if it's not raccoons, it's probably just squirrels."

"Oh, squirrels are the cutest," Cat says. "Especially the little red ones."

"It could be rats," Gum points out.

Cat shivers and glares at him.

"Just saying," Gum says.

Sam leans between Gum and Cat and squints into the darkness beyond the grate. "I can't see anything in there," she says with a sigh.

"Who's got a screwdriver?" Gum says as he pokes at a screw in the corner of the grate. "We can pop this thing right off."

TURN THE PAGE.

"There might be one up there," Sam says. She nods toward the ladder set up under the nearby chandelier. The maintenance worker walks away to a different hallway, and his tools sit on the top of the ladder, unattended.

"Sam and Gum!" Cat says. "We can't just start taking apart the air-conditioning system at the public library."

"Why not?" Gum says. "It's a public library. We're the public. Therefore, it's our library."

"I think a flashlight might work too," Egg says. He takes off his backpack and digs around. "I'm sure I have one in here."

TO USE THE SCREWDRIVER, TURN TO PAGE 53.
TO USE THE FLASHLIGHT, TURN TO PAGE 77.

Cat bounces nervously as she watches Sam climb two rungs up the unattended ladder to reach the box of tools. "This is a very bad idea," Cat says.

"Oh, relax," Sam says. "Here it is." She holds out a yellow-handled screwdriver to Gum, who waits at the bottom of the ladder.

"Thank you," Gum says. "Now, step aside, Cat."

"Gum," Cat says, "put the screwdriver back, we're going to get into—"

"What do you kids think you're doing?!" snaps the maintenance man as he steps into the hall.

Sam freezes just as she steps on the third rung of the ladder.

Gum freezes with the screwdriver raised toward the fancy vent cover.

Egg freezes with the camera halfway to his eye.

Cat covers her mouth with both hands and squeals, her eyes wide and terrified.

"Get down from there," the maintenance man snarls at Sam. "You kids better have a good explanation for this."

TURN THE PAGE.

Sam climbs down quickly.

"We're sorry," Cat says. "I mean, they're sorry."

The maintenance guy looks back and forth between Gum and Sam.

"What exactly were you doing, anyway?" he asks, grabbing the screwdriver from Gum.

He doesn't wait for an answer. "You're with that field trip, aren't you?" he says. "I hate field trips. You kids are always causing trouble of one kind or another."

"We just wanted to catch the vermin in the ducts," Gum says.

"Vermin in the ducts?" the maintenance man asks. His cheeks turn red with fury. "Who says there are vermin in the ducts?!"

"We heard them," Gum says, "and—"

"That's my job," the maintenance man says, "and I can do it just fine without help from a bunch of little kids!"

"Who's little?" Sam says.

TURN THE PAGE.

"Just get back to your field trip," the maintenance man says. "Stay with your group and I won't have to get you in trouble."

"Thank you," Cat says. She takes Gum by the wrist. "Sorry. Thanks. Bye!"

Cat pulls Gum into a big reading room. Sam and Egg follow, though Sam gives the maintenance man one more sneer before she leaves the corridor.

Their classmate Chloe Marshfield passes them heading the other direction with bright blue hair, a pencil behind her ear, and a sketchbook under one arm.

"You're lucky he was nice," Cat says as she drops into a wooden chair at a big table.

"Nice?!" Sam says. She sits on the edge of the table. "That guy?"

Gum sits next to Cat. "Yeah, he was a real saint," Gum says.

Egg puts his camera in his lap and scrolls through today's photos.

"Anything good?" Cat asks.

"Let's see . . . ," he says. "Mr. Spade. The librarian. Sam on a ladder. Gum with a big green bubble blocking his face. Chloe Marshfield drawing in the front entrance. A very angry maintenance man . . ."

"You two could have gotten in big trouble." Cat says.

Sam waves her off. "Ah, Gum and I could handle that guy," she says. "Right, Gum?"

Gum stares straight ahead and doesn't answer.

"Hello?" Sam says. She snaps in front of his face. "Earth to Gum!"

Gum flinches. "Sorry," he says. "I was just thinking."

"Uh-oh," Egg says. "That's usually how things start when we end up in trouble."

"Seriously," Gum says. "Hear me out."

"Go ahead," Sam says, sliding into the chair across from him.

TURN THE PAGE.

"The maintenance man got super angry," he says.

"Of course he did," Cat says. "But he didn't tell on us."

"Right," Gum says. "That's what's so weird. He could have. So why didn't he?"

Sam shrugs. "Maybe Cat's right," she says. "He's nice."

"Didn't seem nice to me," Egg says, digging around in his bag. "Oh, found my flashlight." He holds up the slim, black flashlight.

"I agree with Egg," Gum says. "I think he didn't tell on us because he doesn't want anyone poking around in his business—or in the vents."

"What do you mean?" Sam says. She pulls out her clues notebook and takes the yellow pencil from behind her ear, ready to write.

"He got mad when we said there are critters in the vents," Gum says, "what if there are raccoons or squirrels or mice in the ducts, and the maintenance man knows it?"

"And he's protecting them?" Cat says, smiling. "He is nice!"

"Maybe . . . ," Gum says slowly, "or he knows that this has happened before, and he doesn't want to get fired because it's happening again."

"So he wants to get rid of them on his own," Sam concludes, "so Abdi won't find out and the maintenance man won't get in trouble, and maybe lose his job."

Gum taps his nose. "Exactly," he says.

"Or he's protecting them," Cat says quickly. "Just saying."

"How do we prove it?" Gum says.

"We find the critters," Egg says, "We could check the basement."

"But what if he isn't lying?" Cat says. "It is his job. Maybe he's checked all up and down the vents and hasn't found anything."

To CHECK OTHER VENTS FOR WHAT COULD BE MAKING THAT SOUND, TURN TO PAGE 60.

To HEAD TO THE BASEMENT, TURN TO PAGE 66.

The four friends come down the wide, marble steps near the front entrance.

"We've been wandering for hours," Gum says. He walks as if he's lost in the desert. His shoulders sag. His head droops. His eyelids hang half closed. His jaw chomps slowly on his glowing green gum.

"We've been wandering," Egg says, looking at his watch, "for eight minutes."

"How many vents have we checked so far?" Cat asks.

Sam checks her notebook. "Eleven," she says. "And we've heard scratching at every one of them."

"And voices," Egg says.

"Yup," Sam says as they turn down a wide corridor. "We heard voices at two, footsteps at four, and random banging and stuff at one."

"Oh," Cat says. "We're back here."

They're in the long, old-looking corridor again. The maintenance man is gone now.

At the far end, their classmate Chloe Marshfield sits sideways on the bench under the window.

Chloe's feet are up and she uses her knees like a drafting table to support her sketchbook.

She draws with intensity. Her tongue pokes out from her crooked lips as she works.

"Hi, Chloe," Cat says as the four sleuths stop next to her perch.

"Hi, kitty cat," Chloe says without looking up. "What are you suspicious kids up to?"

Chloe and Cat are friends, but when Cat and her friends are working on a mystery, Chloe teases them. As if the four amateur detectives are the most suspicious people around.

And sometimes they are.

"Not much," Cat says. "Can I see your drawing?"

Chloe lifts her pencil, considers her drawing with her head turned like a confused puppy's, and holds up her sketchbook.

"Is . . . is that me?" Cat says.

"And me!" Gum says.

TURN THE PAGE.

"Yup," Chloe says, putting the book back on her lap. "It's the four of you. I'm thinking of making a comic book about four sleuthing kids who go on field trips and solve crimes."

"Whoa, really?" Sam says, leaning over to get a better look.

"Too out there?" Chloe asks. She pushes her blue bangs off her glasses.

"I think it's brilliant," Egg says. "Let me know if you want to use some of my photos to draw." He gently pats the camera around his neck.

"Thanks!" Chloe says. "I may take you up on that."

"Got that flashlight, Egg?" Sam says.

"Right here," Egg says, handing the flashlight to Sam.

"Thanks," Sam says. "Excuse me, Chloe. I just need to take a peek in here."

"In the vent?" Chloe says. "Why?"

"Oh, you know," Cat says with a smile. "Solving a mystery."

TURN THE PAGE.

"Of course," Chloe says.

"Nothing," Sam says. "And I don't hear anything, either."

"What should you hear?" Chloe asks.

"Scritch scritch," Sam says.

"More like scraatch screetch," Gum corrects.

"No, it's really more like shrssh schwish," Cat tries.

"Have you heard anything like that?" Egg asks.

"Nope," Chloe says with a shake of her head. "But I'll listen more closely while I'm here drawing."

"Okay," Cat says. "Thanks. Sorry to interrupt your comic drawing. We can't wait to see it when it's done."

The four sleuths begin to walk off, but before they get a few yards away, the sound is back.

Scritch schwish scratch screetch!

They stop short. The four of them turn around and look at Chloe.

The tip of her pencil scratches along the toothy surface of her sketch paper.

She makes a mistake and takes up her pink eraser.

Schwish shrssh!

"You don't think . . . ," Cat says.

Sam nods. "I do think," she says. "Chloe's sketching noises carried all around the library through the vent behind her."

Egg snaps a photo of Chloe at work in the window. It's a great shot.

"I guess that mystery is solved," Sam says.

"Abdi the librarian will be so relieved," Cat says.

Gum laughs and says, "So will the maintenance man."

THE END

To follow another path, turn to page 19.

"I don't think we're supposed to be here," Cat says.

The four amateur detectives move quietly along a cool, gray hallway. There are plain, steel doors along both sides of the corridor. It is lit by cold, flickering fluorescent lights and the glowing red of an exit sign.

"I haven't seen anything saying this area is off limits," Gum points out. He walks at the front of the group, eagerly trying—and failing—to open every plain door they pass.

He stops. "Shh," he says, one finger to his lips.

The others stop too.

There are quiet voices around the corner up ahead.

"What if Adbi finds them?" says a girl's voice.

"So what if he does?" says a boy's voice.

"We'll get caught," says the girl.

"No way," says the boy.

"And I'll lose my job here," says the girl.

The four sleuths huddle together. "They must be talking about the critters in the vents," Sam whispers. "Maybe they put them in there."

"Why would they do that?" Cat asks.

"I don't know," Sam says. "Maybe one of them left a vent cover off, and the little guys just climbed into it."

"They're probably talking about something else," Cat says. "And if that girl works here, she's probably about to catch us down here. We'll get in trouble. Let's just go back upstairs!"

To jump around the corner and catch the boy and girl vermin protectors, turn to page 72.

To hurry back upstairs, turn to page 68.

As the four junior detectives are trying to decide what to do, they hear the girl ask, "Do you hear something?"

"No," the boy replies. "You're just nervous."

"No, I heard voices," the girl says, "from around the corner."

The four friends trade panicked glances and take off down the hall for the steps out of the basement.

Sam, the fastest of them, pulls open the heavy door to the stairwell and guides her friends through. "Hurry, hurry!" she orders. She finally grabs Egg by the wrist and pulls him through before letting the door slam closed.

Gum and Sam take the steps two at a time and burst out of the stairwell and into the front entryway of the library—

—and run right into Mr. Spade.

TURN THE PAGE.

"Ah," Mr. Spade says as Egg and Cat, breathless from running, finally emerge from the stairwell too. "Everyone else is already on the bus. I did a head count and we were four short."

He makes a dramatic point of counting Sam, Gum, Egg, and Cat: "One, two, three, and . . . yes. Four. What a coincidence."

"We're sorry, Mr. Spade," Cat says. "We were just—"

"Save it!" Mr. Spade says. "I've heard more than I can take from you private eyes. When we get back to school, we can talk about your next case: the mystery of how much extra homework you four can do in one weekend!"

"But Mr. Spade—" Gum starts.

"No!" Mr. Spade says. "On the bus. Let's go."

Cat, Egg, Sam, and Gum walk slowly at the back of their class and climb onto the bus.

"Just say it," Sam says when they're all seated near one another at the front of the bus, the only seats left for them.

"Yeah," Gum says, glaring at Cat. "Say it."

"Say what?" Cat says.

Egg rolls his eyes. "Say it," he says.

"I don't know what you're talking about," Cat says. Then she says so quietly almost no one can hear her, "Told you so."

THE END

To follow another path, turn to page 19.

"On three," Gum whispers.

His friends nod, and he counts silently: One, two . . .

"Three!" he shouts, and the four sleuths leap around the corner.

It's a boy and girl, about sixteen years old. The girl is Yasmin, the one who scolded Cat for trying to take a book from the hold shelf earlier.

"Ah!" Yasmin screams, startled by the sudden appearance of the amateur detectives. "Don't do that!"

"Who are you?" the boy asks.

"We could ask you the same question!" Gum says.

"So?" the boy says.

"What are you kids doing down here?" Yasmin asks.

"We could ask you the same question!" Gum says.

"Aren't you with the field trip from Mr. Spade's class?" Yasmin asks.

"We could ask you the same question!" Gum repeats.

"Gum," Sam snaps. "Stop saying that."

"Sorry," Gum says.

"Why don't you kids just head back to your field trip," the boy says, "and we'll forget we caught you down here."

"Henry!" Yasmin says. "You don't even work here!"

"Which brings us back to the real question," Sam says. She crosses her arms. She's almost as tall as the sixteen-year-olds. "What do you know about the family of raccoons living in the air conditioner ducts?" Sam says. The words burst from her mouth as fast as a speeding river.

The teens' mouths drop open. "What," Henry asks, "are you talking about?"

Sam squints at him. "Wait, what?" she asks.

Henry and Yasmin look truly shocked.

"I think they really have no idea what you're talking about, Sam," Cat says.

TURN THE PAGE.

"We really have no idea," Yasmin says. "I just volunteer here three mornings a week. I snuck away with Henry for a few minutes. He's my . . . my boyfriend."

"Ohhh . . . ," Gum says, nodding slowly and looking very wise. He puts an arm around Egg. "Come on, guys. Let's leave them alone. They probably want to make smoochies."

Both teens' faces turn red.

"S-sorry," Sam says. She takes Cat by the hand and pulls her away, following Egg and Gum. "We didn't mean to—Sorry!"

The four best friends hurry for the stairs, but Yasmin isn't letting them go that quickly. "Wait a minute!" she shouts after them.

They hear her fast footsteps as she chases after them. "You're still not supposed to be down here!" she says. "You're in trouble!"

"Yasmin!" Henry calls, now also in on the chase. "We're not supposed to be down here either!"

As Gum reaches the door to the stairwell, the door flies open, nearly knocking him backward. It's Abdi the librarian.

"Actually," he says, "none of you are supposed to be down here."

"Abdi!" Yasmin says. "I can explain."

"No need," Abdi says. "We've talked about this. You can't work and hang out with your boyfriend at the same time—unless, Henry, you'd like to volunteer at the library too?"

"Um," Henry says. "Could I?"

Abdi laughs. "We'll talk about it later." He turns his attention to Gum, Egg, Sam, and Cat. "As for you four . . . ," he says.

"We know," Sam says. "We're in big trouble."

"Yup," Gum says. "Cat was right as usual. We shouldn't have come down here."

"Actually," Abdi says, "our basement is where we hold classes and allow community groups to use conference and classrooms. It is indeed open to the public."

TURN THE PAGE.

"Oh," Gum says.

"Then why are we in trouble?" Egg asks.

Abdi crosses his arms and smiles; his eyes twinkle mischievously. "Because," he says, "everyone else in Mr. Spade's sixth-grade class is already on the bus. He's been trying to track you four down."

"Oops," Egg says. He checks his watch. "The time just got away from us."

Gum cries, "And we still haven't solved the mystery!"

THE END

TO FOLLOW ANOTHER PATH, TURN TO PAGE 19.

"See anything?" Sam asks, leaning over Egg's shoulder.

Egg points his small black flashlight's beam into the ductwork. "Not . . . really," he admits. "It's metal. It's rectangular. It's empty."

He sits up straight and switches off the flashlight. "There's really nothing much to see," he says.

"Well," Sam says, "there must be a bunch more grates we can check."

"Yeah," Cat adds. "We're bound to find the raccoon kits in one of them."

"Hey, what are you kids doing?!" asks an angry voice.

The four sleuths look up to find that the maintenance man has returned to his ladder— and also found four kids poking around with a flashlight.

"Nothing!" Sam says. "We're just sitting here."

"You think I didn't see your friend just now," he barks at Sam, "shining that flashlight into my ductwork?"

TURN THE PAGE.

"Your ductwork?" Gum says. "This is a public library, and we're the public, so that makes it our ductwork."

"Not helping, Gum," Cat says out of the corner of her mouth.

"Look, we were just trying to see the raccoons in there," Sam says. "No big deal."

"Raccoons?!" the maintenance man says. "If I've told Abdi once, I've told him a thousand times: we do not have raccoons in our ducts!"

"But we heard them!" Gum protests.

"Oh, and you're experts on raccoons, huh?" the maintenance man says. "Well, I don't think I'd call us experts," Gum says with a shrug. "More like highly experienced hobbyists."

The maintenance man is so mad, he nearly spits. "We'll see about that," he says. "Come with me. We'll talk to your teacher about this."

With that, he crosses his arms and nods toward the big reading room. "Let's go," he orders.

TURN THE PAGE.

The four friends do as they're told and head into the reading room, where Mr. Spade is sitting at a table with Abdi the librarian.

"Uh-oh," Mr. Spade says when he sees Gum, Egg, Cat, and Sam being led along by a very angry-looking maintenance man. "What have they done now?" He stands and adds quickly, "Snooping? Looking for trouble where there is none?"

"Close enough," the maintenance man says. "Just keep them out of my hair and out of the ductwork for the rest of this field trip."

"They won't be able to do any more snooping while they're sitting right here with me and Abdi," Mr. Spade says, "Isn't that right, kids?"

"Yes, Mr. Spade," say Gum, Cat, Sam, and Egg together.

"Looks like the mystery goes unsolved this time," Sam says as she takes a seat at the table. "Phooey."

THE END

TO FOLLOW ANOTHER PATH, TURN TO PAGE 19.

"We made the right choice," Sam says as the four amateur detectives peruse the shelves. "I'm telling you: this case is going to bust the international spy ring wide open."

"Sam," Cat says. "All we have is a scrap of paper that says 'Leo One.' I don't know if this is that important."

"Are you kidding?" Sam says. "It's a code, and if Abdi is right there are scraps of paper like this all over the library."

"Don't spies use tech to send messages?" Egg asks. "Like disguised IP addresses, burner phones, satellite hacking . . . things like that?"

"This isn't a movie, Egg," Sam says. "Real spies rely on good old codes and paper notes. Easy to destroy, no permanent record left online somewhere for the enemy to find, and—"

"Here's one!" Gum announces. He's around the corner from Sam and Egg, in the biographies section.

"What's it say?" Sam asks excitedly as she rounds the corner.

TURN THE PAGE.

Gum hands it over and Sam reads it, "L-E-I. Lee?"

"Lei," Egg corrects her, pronouncing it like "lay." "It's one of those Hawaiian flower necklaces they give you when you get off the plane."

"Hmm," Sam says. She pulls out her clues notebook and takes the pencil from behind her ear. "Maybe a contact in Hawaii. Maybe we should look at the books about Hawaii. We could learn something helpful."

"And if we don't find anything," Egg says, "then what do we do?"

"I say we ask around," Sam says. "Mr. Spade probably knows a lot about Hawaii. Maybe he can give us a clue on these spies."

To look at the books about Hawaii, turn to page 91.
To look for Mr. Spade, continue on to page 83.

Cat, Gum, and Egg follow behind Sam as she rushes from room to room in the old library looking for Mr. Spade.

"There he is," Egg says. "With Anton."

Mr. Spade walks into the room with Anton Gutman, official class bully and all-around stinky head.

"Anton definitely doesn't look too happy," Egg points out.

"Does he ever?" Cat says.

"I think you'll spend the rest of this trip sitting quietly with me in here, Anton," Mr. Spade says.

"I didn't do anything!" Anton protests.

"Perhaps," Mr. Spade says. He sits at one of the big, wooden tables. Anton sits down too and puts his head down.

"What happened?" Sam asks.

"What Anton did to get in trouble is not your concern," Mr. Spade says.

TURN THE PAGE.

"Mr. Spade found a marker in my hoodie pocket, so now he thinks I was planning to tag the bathroom," Anton says.

"Weren't you?" Gum says. "I mean, you usually do."

"No!" Anton says. "At least, no one can prove I was going to."

"Markers are not allowed on field trips," Mr. Spade says. He turns to Anton. "And anyone who forgets it can sit with Ms. Gilgamesh's class while we're on our next field trip."

The four sleuths exit the room and regroup in the hallway. Sam gives her friends a look that she's onto something.

"What are you thinking, Sam?" Cat asks.

"Did you hear what Anton got busted for?" Sam asks.

"His marker," Gum says. "Hardly the first time."

"Take a look at this," Sam says. She pulls a scrap of paper from her pocket.

"L-E-I," Egg says.

"We know," Gum says.

"In black marker," Sam adds.

Her three friends stop short, mouths open. "It was Anton," they say together.

Sam nods.

TO CONFRONT ANTON WITH THE EVIDENCE, TURN TO PAGE 86.

TO FIND ABDI AND ACCUSE ANTON, TURN TO PAGE 88.

"Let's confront Anton. He's still sitting with Mr. Spade," Egg says as the sleuths return to the reading room.

"That's as close as he can come to suspension while we're on a field trip," Gum says. "You know how much trouble he got in for graffiti in the past."

Cat nods sadly. "Poor Anton," she says. "Imagine how troubled his little heart must be." Cat's caring for all creatures did not stop at the human race, even a human as awful as Anton Gutman.

"Your kindness never ceases to amaze me." Egg says to Cat.

"I'm pretty sure Anton's just a jerk." Sam says.

The four sleuths walk up to Mr. Spade's table. "Can we talk to Anton, Mr. Spade?" Sam asks.

"It's a free country," Mr. Spade says without lifting his eyes from the book he's reading.

"I don't have to talk to you, though," Anton says pointedly to Sam. "Dorktectives."

"Did you write this?" Sam says. She lays the 'LEO I' scrap of paper on the table in front of him.

"One-oh-three-seven?" Anton says.

"Wait, it's upside down," Sam says. She turns the paper. "There."

"LEO I," Anton says. "No, I didn't write that. Now scram."

"In fact," Mr. Spade says as he stands up, "scram directly on to the bus."

"What?" Sam says. "Already? But the spies are still out there! They'll probably take down the government!"

"I don't know what you're ranting about, Archer," Mr. Spade says to Sam. "But the field trip is over."

"Darn it," Sam says, shoving her hands into her pocket. She and her three best friends head to the front.

THE END

TO FOLLOW ANOTHER PATH, TURN TO PAGE 19.

"Abdi will probably be at the desk in the reading room," Cat suggests.

She and her three best friends hurry back into the reading room. Anton glares at them as they enter.

"He knows we're onto him!" Sam tells her friends.

Abdi stands behind the big research desk. "Hello," he says as they step up to the counter. "Something you need help with?"

"Not exactly," Cat says. "We might be able to help you, though."

"We are here to tell you who's been leaving those pesky notes all over the library!" Sam says.

"Oh really?" Abdi says. "Tell me what you've learned."

Sam plops the 'L-E-O I' note on the table. "Written in black marker," she says. "Our classmate over there"—she thumbs over her shoulder at Anton Gutman— "was busted with a black marker just a few minutes ago."

"Busted?" Abdi asks.

"Anton isn't allowed to carry black markers," Gum says. "It's a long story."

"He always writes his name on bathroom walls," Egg says.

Gum shrugs. "I guess it wasn't that long," he admits.

"And this Anton character," Abdi says, "does he spend a lot of time at the central library?"

"Well, no," Sam says. "Probably not. But he's been here all morning . . . and with a black marker."

Abdi laughs lightly. "Interesting theory, kids," he says, "but I'm happy to say your friend Anton is not guilty. The notes have been appearing for weeks . . . since right around when the new crop of volunteers started."

"Oh," Sam says.

"You four ready to hit the road?" asks Mr. Spade as he steps up behind them. "Check out any books you've chosen quickly, please."

TURN THE PAGE.

With that, he walks off to gather their classmates.

"We're out of time already?" Sam says.

"Time sure flies when you're having fun," Egg says.

"And apparently when you're not, too," Gum adds.

The two boys hurry ahead toward the exit.

"I don't know how they can joke," Sam says as she walks beside Cat. "Most of the morning on a field trip, and we didn't solve the mystery."

Cat pats her friend on the back. "Don't worry, Sam," she says. "Just think, if it wasn't Anton, it means it might really be an international spy ring."

"That's true!" Sam says, brightening a little. "Boy, wait till I tell Grandpa when I get home. He'll be so jealous."

THE END

TO FOLLOW ANOTHER PATH, TURN TO PAGE 19.

"Books about the states are over here," Gum says as he leads his friends between shelves, deep in the nonfiction adult books.

"Since when do you know how to find anything at the library?" Cat asks.

"It's pretty simple," Gum says with a shrug. "And if you can't remember the catalog codes, it says at the end of every row what's down that row."

"Huh," Sam says, peeking around the end of a bookshelf. "'United States'. Says it right there."

"Hey, look at this!" Egg says. He's stooped over in front of the small selection of books about Hawaii and pulls out another slip of paper.

"Another code?" Sam asks, running over and snatching the paper.

"Excuse me," Egg says.

"Sorry," Sam says, blushing a little. "I'm a little excited."

"I see that," Egg says. He sighs. "So what does it say?"

TURN THE PAGE.

"It says 'lie'," Sam says.

"Like, the opposite of truth?" Cat asks.

Sam hands her the paper. "Yup," Sam says. "All caps, thick black marker, just like the others."

L-I-E

"No it doesn't," Gum says. He stands in front of Cat and looks at the paper in her hand.

"Um, yes it does," Cat says.

Gum shakes his hand. "It says three-one-seven," Gum says.

"You're looking at it upside-down," Sam says. She takes the paper, flips it over, and shows it to Gum. "See?"

"How do we know you're not looking at it upside-down?" Gum says. "Maybe it's numbers, not letters. Aren't codes often numbers instead of letters?"

"That's ridiculous," Sam says. She turns her back on him and crosses her arms.

TURN THE PAGE.

"Ridiculous like a fox," Gum says, tapping his skull with one finger.

"Looks like Cat and I will have to settle this," Egg says.

"Well . . . ," Cat says, glancing quickly from Gum to Sam and back again. "I guess I think it looks like letters."

Gum gasps.

"I'm sorry!" Cat says. "It just looks like letters to me."

"What do you say, Egg?" Sam asks.

"Let me see the other note," Egg says.

Sam hands the first note over.

Egg turns it in his hands. "It says 'lei,'" he says.

"Aha!" Sam says. "Then it's three to one for letters."

"But," Egg continues, "it also says one-three-seven."

L-E-I

137

"Oh, here we go again," Sam says. "Who would ever make a three like that? All blocky and everything?"

"My mom's clock radio," Gum says.

Sam sneers at him.

TO AGREE WITH CAT AND SAM THAT THE PAPER SHOWS LETTERS, TURN TO PAGE 96.

TO AGREE WITH EGG THAT IT SHOWS LETTERS AND NUMBERS, TURN TO PAGE 99.

"We have 'Leo one,'" Sam says as she paces before her friends, who are seated at a big table in the reading room, "'lie,' and 'lei.'"

She's been pacing for twenty minutes.

"That's a lot of Ls," Gum points out. He's leaning his elbows on the table and his chin on his fists. "Also my gum is out of flavor and I'm bored."

"And a lot of Is and Es," Egg adds. He takes a photo of Sam as she paces—the tenth photo he's taken so far of the trip.

"True," Sam says. She stops and sits next to Cat. "Maybe that's important."

"It might be 'LEO I,' remember," Cat reminds her. "Even more Is."

"And one O," Gum says.

"So the contact must be called Leo," Sam says.

"Or that's just a code name," Gum says.

Sam drops back into her chair and slumps.

Mr. Spade walks up to their table.

"All right, gang," Mr. Spade says. "Time to start gathering at the front to get back on the bus."

"Already?" Sam says. "But we haven't even solved—I mean, I haven't picked out a book yet."

"Sorry!" Mr. Spade says. "Head to the front, please. Head count time."

Their teacher heads off to find the rest of the class.

"Don't feel too bad, Sam," Cat says, patting her friend on the back. "An international spy ring might be out of our league for now, but someday we'll be real PIs. Then we'll get 'em."

Ahead of them, the young library volunteer Yasmin is pushing a metal cart of books to be reshelved. A slip of paper falls out of her back pocket.

"Hey!" Gum says. He runs ahead and picks up the paper. "You dropped this."

Before she can grab it back from him, he scans the little note. "SOS?" Gum reads aloud.

TURN THE PAGE.

"Give me that!" Yasmin snaps, snatching the paper from his fingers.

She shoves it into her back pocket.

Sam's eyes go wide. "It's you!" she says, pointing accusingly at Yasmin. "You're the spy!"

"I'm what?" Yasmin says.

"I should have known!" Sam rants as Cat grabs her by the arm and pulls her toward the exit.

"Sorry," Cat says. "She's had a tough day."

Gum and Egg hurry after them.

"It is her!" Sam says. "It has to be!"

But it's too late, and Mr. Spade ushers the sleuths onto the bus. The mystery remains unsolved.

THE END

To follow another path, turn to page 19.

"What could it mean?" Sam says, pacing in front of a table in the reading room. Her three best friends sit at the table, each of them with a scrap of paper and a tiny pencil.

"'LEO I'," Egg says, "is 'one-zero-three-seven.'"

"And 'LEI,'" Gum says, "is 'one-three-seven.'"

Sam replies, "And 'LIE' is 'three-one-seven.' But what does it mean?"

"Locker combos?" Cat suggests. "They're usually three digits."

"But 'LEO I' is four digits," Egg points out. "One-zero-three-seven."

"We're missing something," Sam says.

"Well, we better hurry," Egg says. "It's already after ten."

"Wait," Sam says. "It's ten what?"

"Um," Egg says, looking at his watch again. "It's 10:17, to be exact. Why?"

"You mean twenty minutes before 10:37?" Sam shouts.

TURN THE PAGE.

"I guess," Egg says. "Why . . . oh!"

"Wait, what?" Gum says.

"I get it too!" Cat says. She jumps from her seat. "10:37! 1:37! And 3:17!"

"You got it!" Sam says. The two girls grab each other's hands and jump up and down in celebration.

"Whoa, whoa, whoa!" Gum says. "What are you talking about?"

"Don't you see?" Sam says. "All of the notes are not just words. They're also times of day."

Gum stares at her blankly and then it clicks. He grins and nods. "I get it!" he says.

"We solved it!" Sam says.

"Did we?" Egg says. "We may have cracked the code, but so what? What do we know about these times of day?"

"Oh," Sam says. She deflates and sits down again.

"This part I think I know," Gum says.

"We found one note about something Hawaiian, right? And then we went to the Hawaii books and found—"

"Another note!" Sam says.

"So if we go to the books about lies, we'll find another note?" Egg says.

"Are there books about lies?" Cat asks.

"There must be," Sam says.

"How about books on Leo I?" Egg suggests.

"At least it's someplace to start," Cat says. "Come on."

Cat leads her friends to the catalog computer and types in "Leo I."

There are dozens of hits, but the first one is—

"Leo the First," Cat reads aloud.

"Was he a king?" Gum asks.

Cat shakes her head. "He was a pope," she says. "There are two books all about him in biographies."

Turn the page.

"Ah!" Gum says. "That's where I found the 'LEI' note!"

"Okay," Egg says. "So if the 'LEO I' note is also the 10:37 note, we should hurry. Our spies might be there at any moment."

***

"No running in the library!" shouts a maintenance man as Sam, Egg, Gum, and Cat sprint along the wide main corridor.

"This way!" Gum says. His sneakers squeak on the hardwood as he careens into the biographies section. It's 10:35.

"This way," Gum says, leading his friends among the stacks. "I found it over here—"

Gum stops short. His three friends nearly barrel into him.

"Can I help you?" says a boy. He's about sixteen and a bit taller than Sam. He stands in front of the books on Leo the First as if protecting them.

"Are you the spy?" Sam says.

"The spy?" the boy says. "Look, don't include me in whatever silly make-believe game you're playing, okay?"

"You're not fooling anyone," Sam says, striding up to the boy. "Are we supposed to believe it's a coincidence that you're standing right here with the books about Pope Leo the First?"

The boy's eyes go wide. "How did you—,"

"Then it's true," Gum says. "You are the spy."

"I'm not a spy," the boy hisses at them. "Now get out of here before—"

"Henry?" says a girl's voice. A moment later Yasmin, the young library volunteer, appears in the aisle. "Who are these kids?"

"You're late, Yas," Henry says. "And I have no idea how, but I think they found my note."

Yasmin covers her face with her hands. "Oh no," she says. "I'm totally getting fired."

"I told you not to leave the note where you find it!" Henry says.

TURN THE PAGE.

"Well I couldn't just take it with me," Yasmin argues. "What if Mr. Burhan found it on me? Then he'd know what we've been doing!"

"What have you been doing?" Egg asks.

"Secret spies?" Sam suggests.

"What?" Yasmin says. "No! Henry is my boyfriend."

The four sleuths stare at the two teens.

"I'm not allowed to socialize during volunteer hours," Yasmin says, "but we just can't bear to not see each other."

"And since I volunteer the same mornings just down the block at the animal shelter," Henry says, "I have to come by to secretly see Yasmin a few times every day."

"Like at 10:37," Egg puts in. "Or Leo the First."

Henry shrugs and smiles. "Yeah," he says.

Yasmin puts an arm around her boyfriend's waist. "My idea. Pretty brilliant, huh?"

TURN THE PAGE.

"Yeah, you're a criminal genius," Sam says, rolling her eyes.

"It did take us a while to figure it all out," Gum says.

"You won't tell on us, will you?" Yasmin says. "I'd for sure lose my position here, and so would Henry."

"And we need these volunteer jobs for our transcripts," Henry adds, "so we can go to college together."

"And then get married," Yasmin says with a sigh.

"Okay, okay," Gum says, covering his ears. "I've heard enough." With that, he walks away. His friends follow.

"It's probably time to get back on the bus," Egg says.

"And hey," Cat says, patting Sam on the back. "We solved the mystery!"

"It wasn't exactly an international spy group, though, was it?" Sam says.

Gum shrugs and blows a bubble. "Good practice, though," he says. "You'll be busting international spies any day now. You wait."

Sam laughs, and together the four friends walk out of the library and climb onto the bus to head back to school.

THE END

TO FOLLOW ANOTHER PATH, TURN TO PAGE 19.

literary news

MYSTERIOUS WRITER REVEALED!

Steve Brezenoff is the author of the Field Trip Mysteries, the Museum Mysteries, and the Ravens Pass series of thrillers, as well as three novels for older readers. Steve lives in Minneapolis, Minnesota, with his wife, Beth, and their two children, Sam and Etta.

arts & entertainment

ARTIST IS KEY TO SOLVING MYSTERY, SAY POLICE

Marcos Calo lives happily in A Coruña, Spain, with his wife, Patricia (who is also an illustrator), and their daughter, Claudia. When Marcos and Patricia aren't drawing, they like to go on long walks by the sea. They also watch a lot of films and eat Nutella™ sandwiches. Yum!

A Detective's Dictionary

amateur — something done by people who play for fun, not money

atrium — a large room inside a building with an open or glass ceiling

biography — a book that tells the life story of someone other than the author

careen — to sway from side to side

chandelier — a light fixture that hangs from the ceiling and is lit by many small lights

flutter — to move back and forth quickly

patron — people who use a library or other facility

pamphlet — a small booklet

vermin — Any small animals or insects that are difficult to get rid of

vigor — great energy or physical strength of body or mind

volunteer — a person who chooses to do work without pay

FURTHER INVESTIGATIONS

CASE #YCSFTMTLSSI9

1. Sam is eager to find suspects, but this sometimes leads her to call out the wrong people. Talk about a time in the story when she upsets someone by naming them as a suspect.

2. Both the Field Trip Mysteries gang and Chloe go off on their own during the trip to the library, but only the gang gets into trouble with Mr. Spade. Why do you think Chloe avoids trouble?

3. The Field Trip Mysteries gang goes to many different places. What part of the library would you be most interested in visiting?

IN YOUR OWN DETECTIVE'S NOTEBOOK . . .

1. Put yourself in Cat's shoes and write a letter from her perspective to a member of M.E.S.S. explaining why the Elves and Spells books aren't as bad as they say.

2. The detectives think spies are sending the mysterious codes they find in the library, but find out they're wrong. Write a version of the story where they find out that it is spies sending secret messages to each other.

3. The detectives mess with the maintenance man's grates while searching for the mysterious sounds. Write a letter from all four of them to the maintenance man. Make sure that each character says something to him.

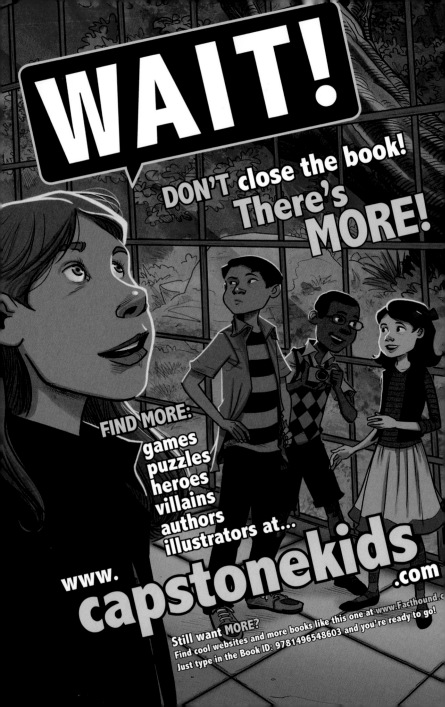